For Jana Novotny Hunter

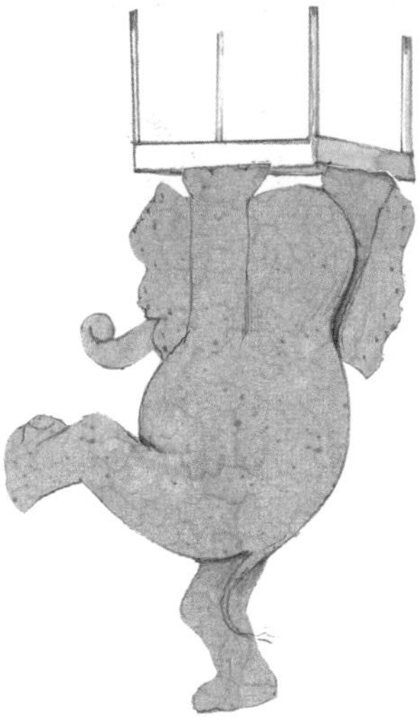

First published in Great Britain in
2004 by Frances Lincoln Children's Books

Library of Congress Cataloging-in-Publication Data available

0-439-73967-5
10 9 8 7 6 5 4 3 2 1 05 06 07 08 09
Printed in Singapore
First Scholastic edition, July 2005
Book design by Venice Shone
and Alison Klapthor

When an Elephant Comes to School

Jan Ormerod

Orchard Books ☆ New York
An Imprint of Scholastic Inc.

Morning Time

When an elephant
comes to school . . .

. . . he may be a bit shy at first. A special friend can show him where to put his lunch box.

Show ☆ him the bathroom right away.

Sharing

Friends are very important to an elephant.

He likes to talk to his friends.

He loves to play.

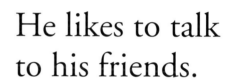

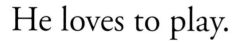

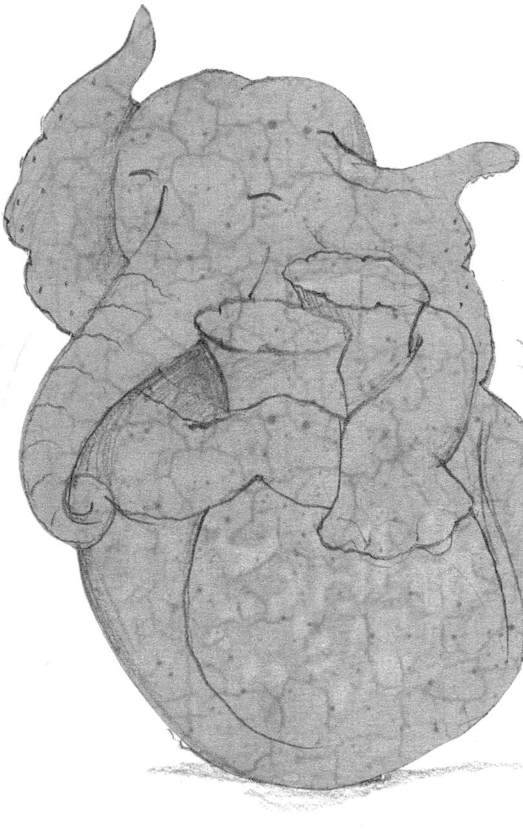

An elephant
wants to join
in everything.

An elephant
needs lots
of love and
hugs.

Arts and Crafts

An elephant loves . . .

paint,

water,

A plastic apron is a good idea. ☆

glue,

and sand.

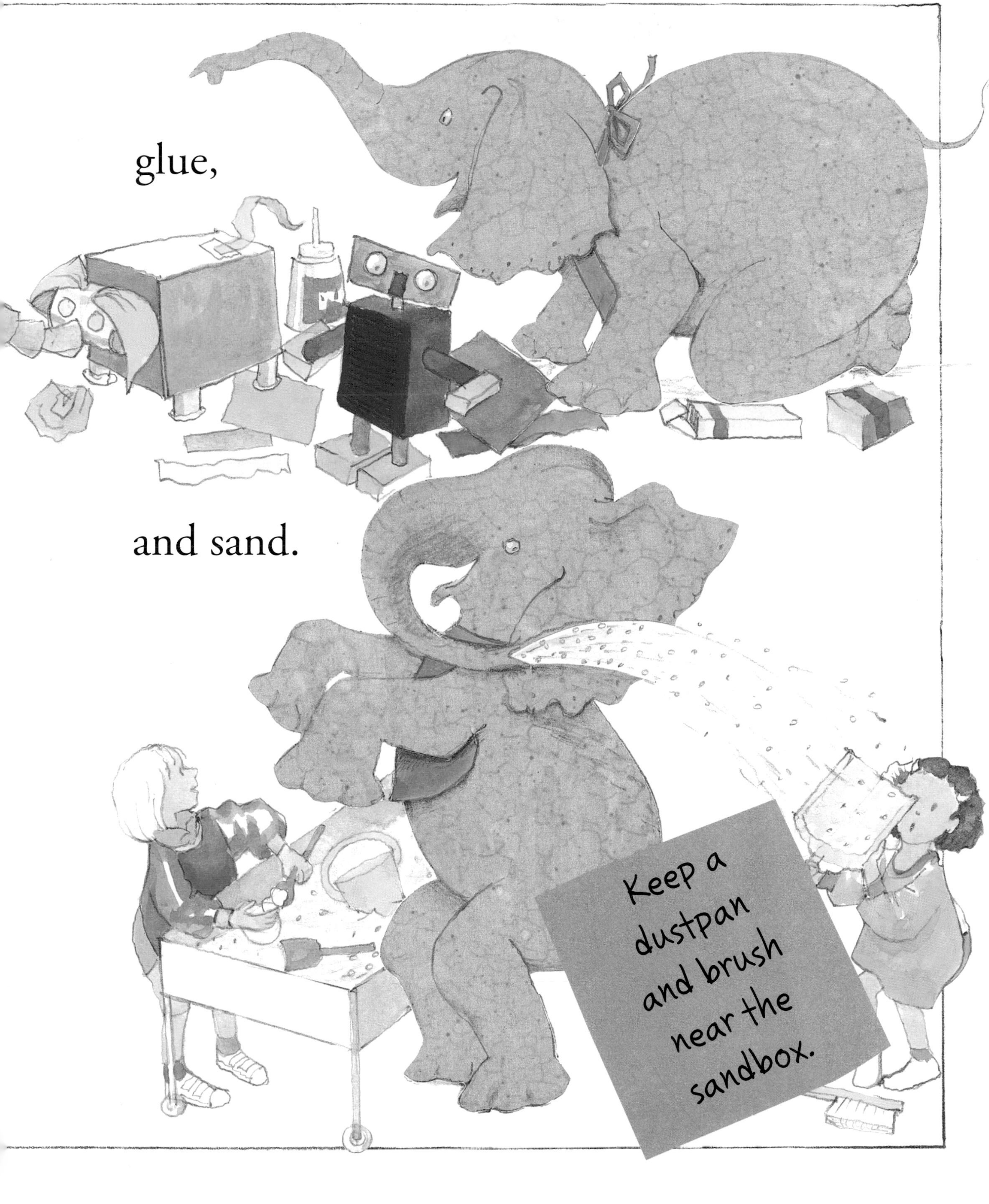
Keep a dustpan and brush near the sandbox.

HELPING

An elephant loves to carry things . . .

. . . especially his friends.

How and Why?

An elephant loves to experiment.

WATCH OUT!

A long trunk works better than a straw!

WHOOPS!

An elephant can be a bit clumsy . . .

. . . and elephants
are not very brave.

When he falls,
make a big
fuss over
him.

LUNCH

An elephant loves to eat.

Take
an extra
sandwich.

He likes cake, bananas,
and lemonade best of all.

PLAYING

Elephants are good at doing tricks with a ball.

Don't let an elephant step on your toes. ☆

But . . .

elephants are NOT
good at sharing.

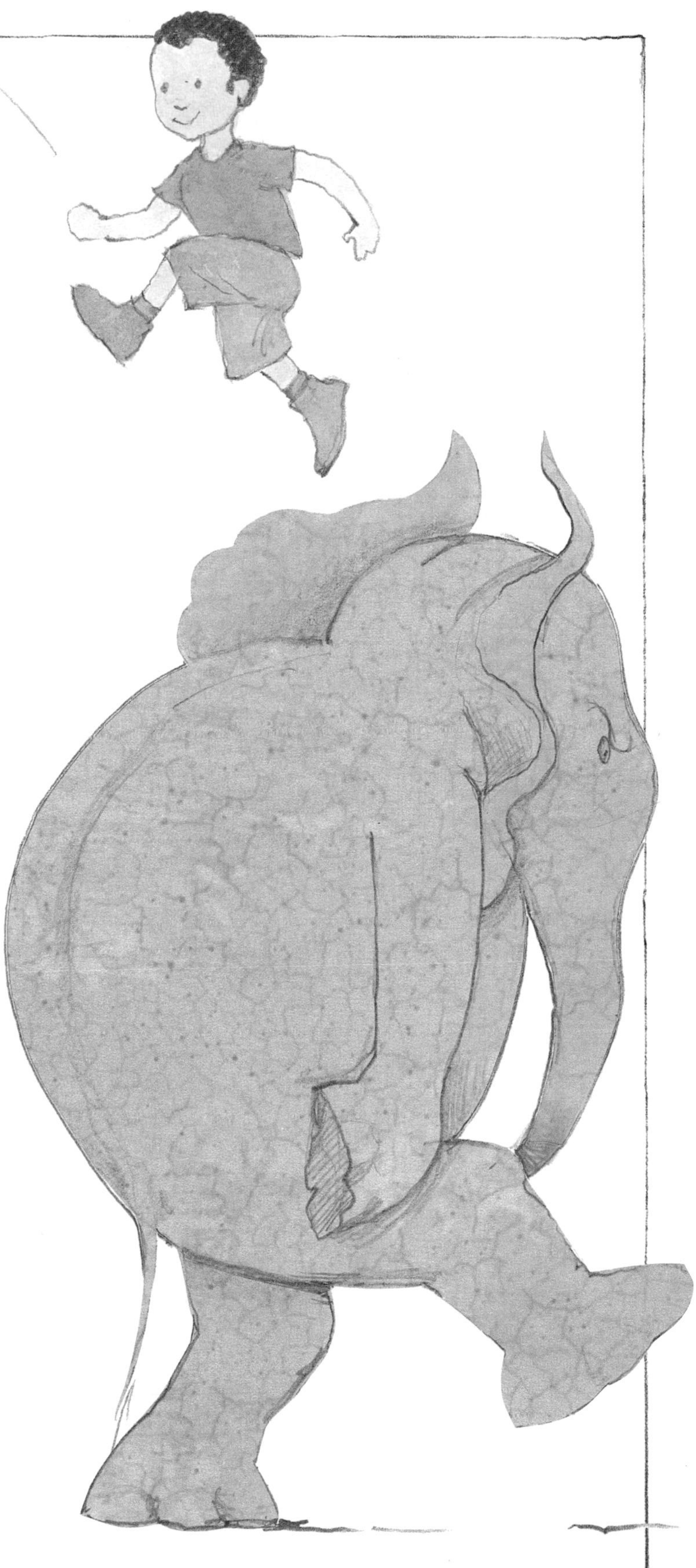

QUIET TIME

If he gets angry,
he is probably
tired and thirsty.

An elephant needs
lots and lots of rest.

Quiet time with a book
and a good friend
is a nice idea.

He likes
stories
about other
elephants.

MOVEMENT

An elephant loves music.
He likes to dance . . .

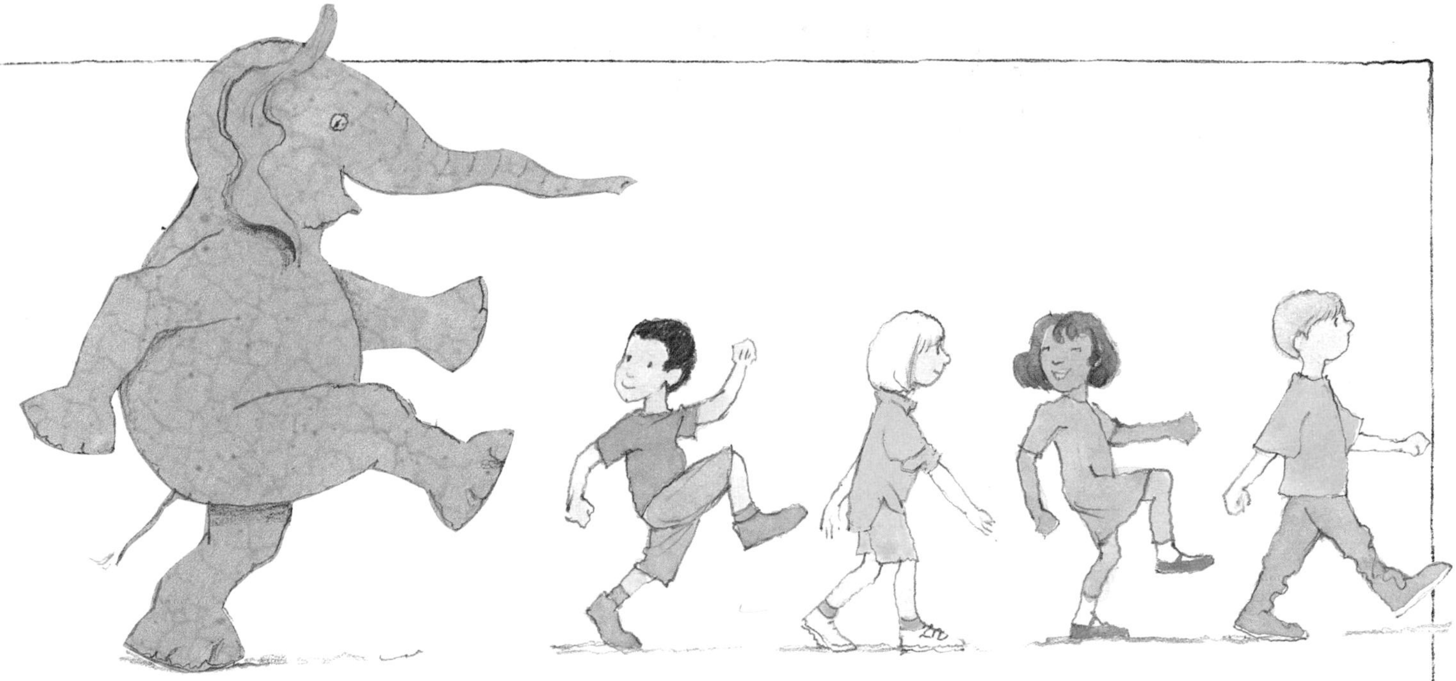

. . . and march.

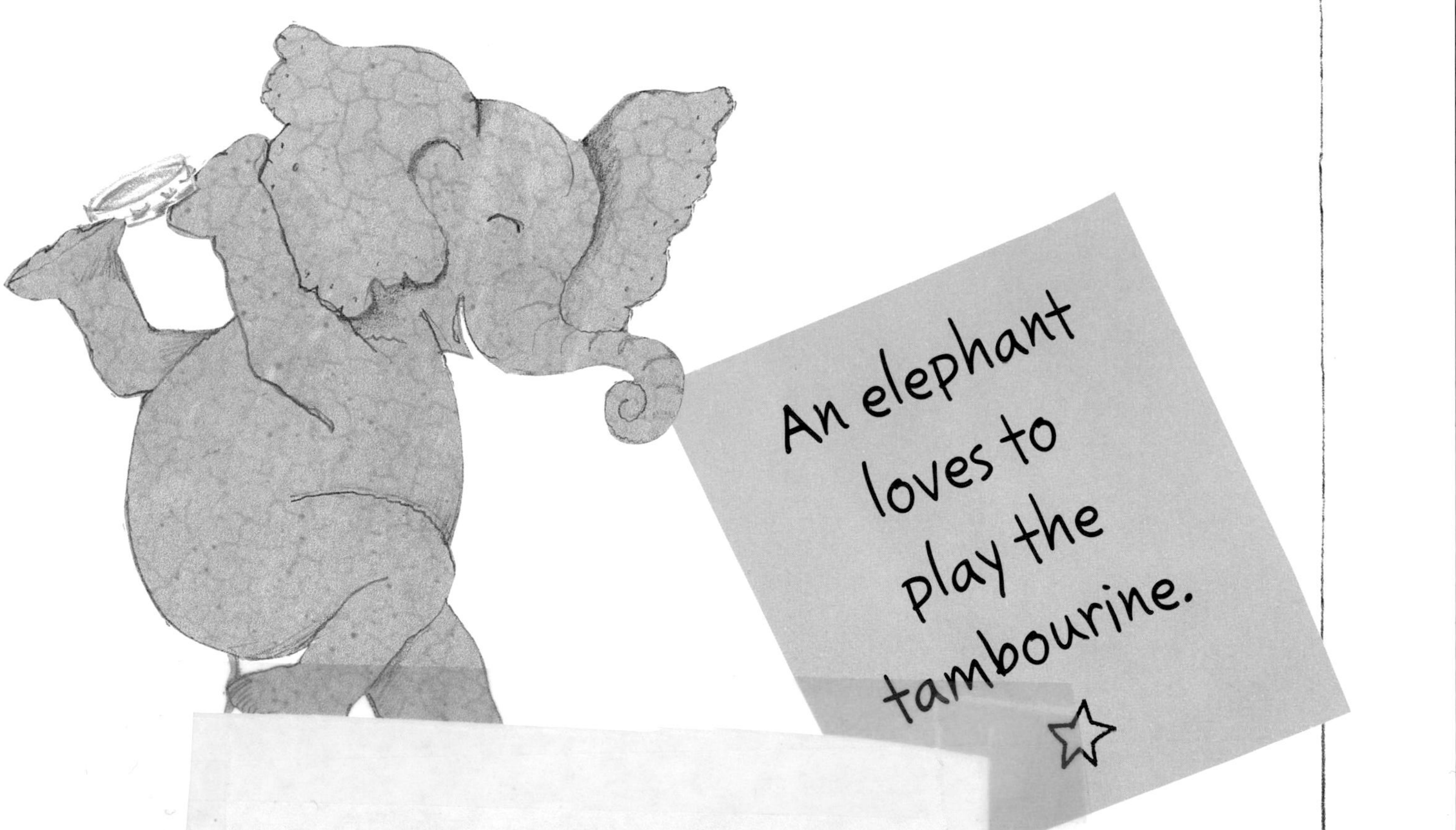
An elephant loves to play the tambourine.

STORYTELLING

An elephant loves a funny story . . .

Have a big box of tissues ready.

. . . but a sad story makes him cry.

He likes to make up his own stories.

BYE-BYE

When an elephant comes to school, he loves to make friends and have fun learning.

And he loves to see his mommy at the end of the day.

"See you tomorrow, Elephant!"